D1061675

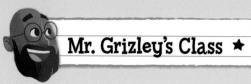

Nicole's

Secret

by Bryan Patrick Avery   illustrated by Arief Putra

PICTURE WINDOW BOOKS
a capstone imprint

Published by Picture Window Books, an imprint of Capstone.
1710 Roe Crest Drive
North Mankato, Minnesota 56003
capstonepub.com

Library of Congress Cataloging-in-Publication Data is available on the Library of Congress website.

ISBN: 9781666339062 (hardcover)
ISBN: 9781666339079 (paperback)
ISBN: 9781666339086 (eBook PDF)

Summary: Nicole's latest robot creation threw a ball right through a window. No one knows how the window got broken, and Nicole decides to keep the accident to herself. But when she realizes the broken window has upset her classmates, she has second thoughts.

Designed by Dina Her

Printed and bound in the USA. PO4882

TABLE OF CONTENTS

Cecilia Gomez

Mr. Grizley's Class ★

Shaw Quinn

Emily Kim

Mordecai Foster

Nathan Wu

Ashok Aparnam

Ryan Clayborn

Rahma Abdi

Nicole Washington

Alijah Wilson

Suddha Agarwal

Chad Werner

Semira Madani

Pierre Boucher

Zoe Charmichael

Dmitry Orloff

Camila Jennings

Madison Tanaka

Annie Barberra

Bobby Lewis

CHAPTER 1

A Big Problem

Nicole couldn't wait to show off BEE, her new robot creation.

She got to school early.
No one was around.

"Okay, BEE," Nicole said.
"Let's play catch!"

BEE beeped. With its robotic arm, BEE scooped a ball out of a small basket. Then, it tossed the ball to Nicole. Nicole caught the ball and grinned.

"Okay, BEE. Throw me another ball," she said.

BEE tossed another ball. Nicole caught it.

"Great job," she said. "My friends are going to love you."

Nicole put the balls back in
the basket.

"Okay, BEE," she said. "Take
a break."

BEE beeped and scooped
another ball. The robot threw
the ball. It hit a trash can with
a thunk.

"Stop!" Nicole shouted.

BEE threw another ball.

It sailed across the playground.

BEE spun in circles. It threw balls all over the place. One of the balls crashed through the window of Mr. Grizley's class! Then, BEE shut down.

Nicole looked around.

She didn't see anyone.

She grabbed BEE and hid
the robot in the bushes near
her classroom. Then, she heard
Mr. Grizley's voice.

CHAPTER 2

The Lie

"What happened here?" Mr. Grizley asked.

Nicole's heart raced. "Um," she mumbled.

"It looks like someone threw something through the window," Mr. Grizley said.

"You didn't see who did this?" Nicole asked.

Mr. Grizley shook his head. "No," he said. "Did you?"

Nicole didn't want to get into trouble. She decided to lie.

"No," she said. "It was like that when I got here."

Nicole followed Mr. Grizley into the classroom.

The ball had broken the window, knocked over a plant, and hit the art supplies shelf. Glass, dirt, and paint were all over the floor.

Mr. Grizley sighed.

"I'll call the office to ask for some supplies so we can clean up this mess," he said.

The rest of the class showed up. Mr. Grizley explained what happened. The class got to work cleaning up.

"Who would do this to our class?" Pierre asked.

"Yeah," Zoe said. "Why would someone want to be mean to us?"

"I hope this was just an accident," Mr. Grizley said. "Someone will probably admit to it soon. When they do, we'll all feel better."

Nicole's stomach hurt.

"What if they're too scared to admit it?" she asked.

CHAPTER 3

The Truth

The class finished cleaning up and took their seats.

"I'm worried," Ryan said. "Is it safe for us to be here?"

"What if whoever did this comes back and throws something while we're here?" Alijah asked.

"We could get hurt," Ryan said.

"It's okay to be a little worried and upset," Mr. Grizley said. "I am too. But I don't think we're in any danger."

Nicole looked at her classmates. She took a deep breath and raised her hand.

"Mr. Grizley," she said. "I think I can explain."

Everyone turned to look at Nicole.

"May I please go outside and get something?" she asked.

Mr. Grizley frowned. He walked to the door with Nicole. She stepped outside and came back in carrying BEE.

"My robot threw the ball through the window," she explained. "I'm really sorry."

Mr. Grizley put a hand on Nicole's shoulder.

"Thank you for telling the truth," he said with a smile.

"Are you mad?" Nicole asked.

Mr. Grizley shook his head.

"No," he said. "It was an
accident. I think we all feel
better knowing what happened."

"Telling the truth made me
feel better too," Nicole said.

"Can we play with your robot?" Alijah asked.

The class laughed. Nicole grinned.

"Maybe after I make a few repairs."

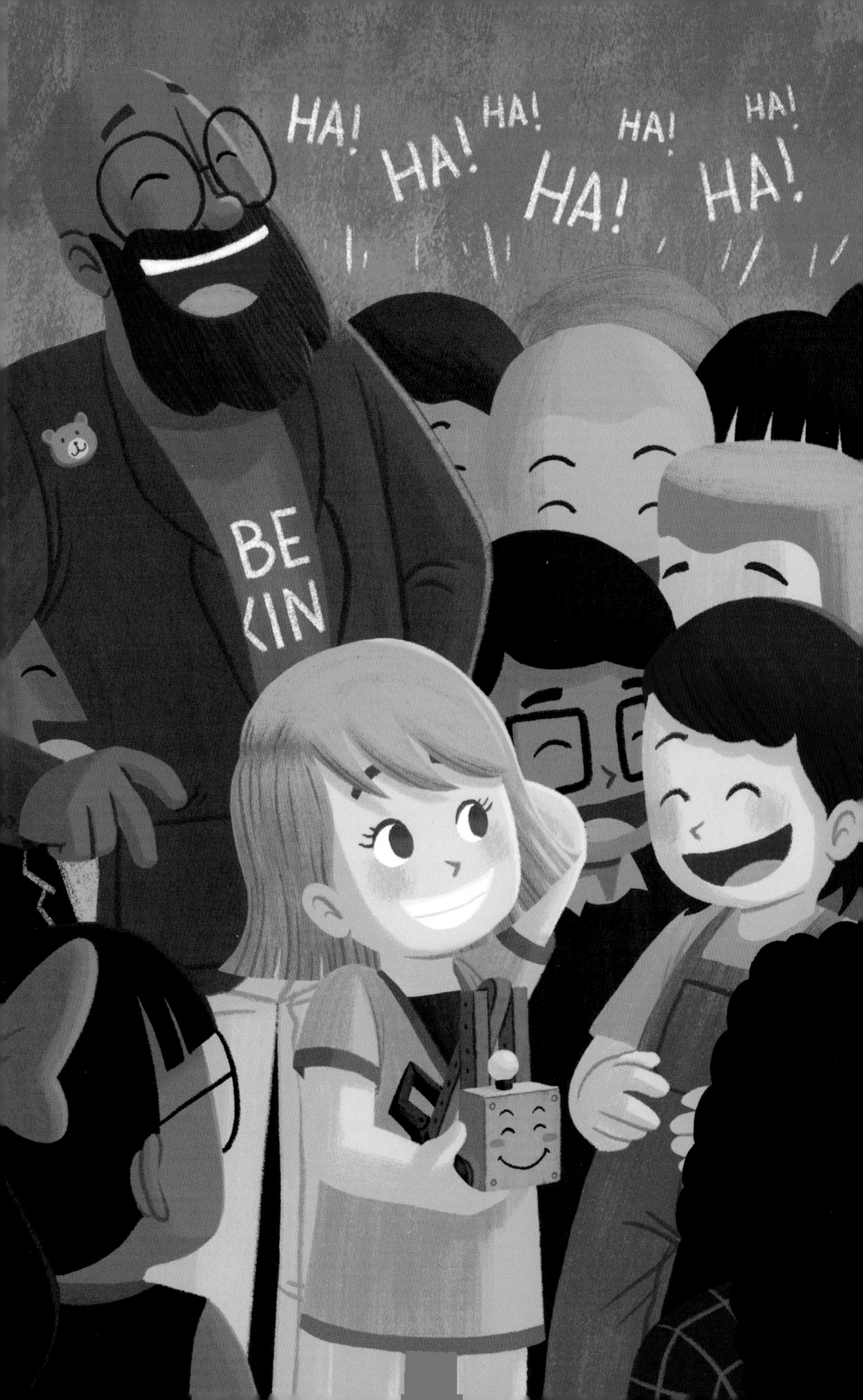
HA!
HA!
HA!
HA!
HA!
HA!
HA!
BE

LET'S PRACTICE HONESTY

Being honest isn't always easy. Sometimes, we are scared we will get in trouble. Or we might worry about what others think of us. Because honesty can sometimes be hard, it helps to remind ourselves to be honest. For this activity, we're going to create a poster to remind us to try to always be honest.

WHAT YOU NEED:
- white or colored paper
- pen or pencil (in your favorite color)
- push pins or tape

WHAT YOU DO:
1. At the top of the page, write "Honest?" Make it nice and big, but leave room to write below it.

2. Below "Honest?" write "Yes" on the left side of the paper. Write "No" on the right side.

3. Below "No" list several actions that are not honest. For example, you could write "Hiding a dish I broke" or "Saying my work is done when it isn't" or "Taking something without asking." These are just examples. Be sure to come up with some of your own as well.

4. Below "Yes" list several actions that are honest. "Telling my dad I lost my jacket" and "Asking before I use my sister's art supplies" are good examples. Add some of your own as well.

5. Decorate your poster using your favorite colors and designs. Then hang it (with a grown-up's permission) someplace you'll see it often.

Remember to read the poster from time to time, and think about the difference between being honest and being dishonest.

GLOSSARY

accident (AK-suh-duhnt)—a sudden and unexpected event that leads to loss or injury

creation (kree-AY-shuhn)—something that has been made or built

repair (ri-PAIR)—to make something work again

robotic (row-BAH-tic)—related to robots, machines that do jobs usually done by humans

sigh (SYE)—to let out a breath because you feel sad, tired, or relieved

supply (suh-PLY)—an item needed to do a job

worry (WUR-ee)—to feel upset or very concerned

TALK ABOUT IT

1. Nicole's robot, BEE, malfunctioned and threw a ball through the classroom window. Have you ever had an accident that broke something? What did you do?

2. Why did Nicole hide BEE in the bushes?

3. Nicole eventually decides to be honest about the accident. What do you think helped her make that decision?

WRITE ABOUT IT

1. When Mr. Grizley asks Nicole if she knows who broke the window, Nicole decides to lie. Have you ever been dishonest about something? How did being dishonest make you feel? Write about it.

2. Write a paragraph describing Nicole's robot.

3. Imagine Mr. Grizley had not allowed Nicole to go outside. Write what happens next.

ABOUT THE AUTHOR

Bryan Patrick Avery discovered his love of reading and writing at an early age when he received his first Bobbsey Twins mystery. He writes picture books, chapter books, middle grade, and graphic novels. He is the author of the picture book *The Freeman Field Photograph*, as well as "The Magic Day Mystery" in *Super Puzzletastic Mysteries*. Bryan lives in northern California with his family.

ABOUT THE ILLUSTRATOR

Arief Putra loves working and drawing in his home studio at the corner of Yogyakarta city in Indonesia. He enjoys coffee, cooking, space documentaries, and solving the Rubik's Cube. Living in a small house in a rural area with his wife and two sons, Arief has a big dream to spread positivity around the world through his art.